Ian Whybrow Ed Eaves

Say Hello
to the
Baby Animals!

MACMILLAN CHILDREN'S BOOKS

KU-759-710

Say Hello
to the
Baby Animals!

This baby lion is ready to go.
He wants to find his friends and say hello.

Baby giraffe looks hungry to me,
Licking the leaves that grow on the tree.

Hello, baby giraffe!

Lick, lick, lick!

I can see a funny face. Can you see it, too?
It's a baby monkey and he's waving at you!

Hello, baby monkey!

Oo, oo, oo!

Baby hippopotamus loves to keep cool.
What a lot of noise when he jumps in the pool!

These little zebras love to run around.
Their hooves click-clack on the hard dry ground.

Hello, baby zebras!

Click-clack, click-clack!

Who's this going squawk, squawk, squawk?
It's a baby parrot and he loves to talk.

Hello, baby parrot!

Squawk, squawk, squawk!

This baby elephant is having fun,
Squirting mud at everyone.

Hello, baby elephant!

Squirt, squirt, squirt!

Here's a baby leopard, walking down the track.
Give him a roar and he'll roar back!

What a lot of babies, my, oh my!
It must be time to say goodbye.

Goodbye, baby monkey!
Oo, oo, oo!

Goodbye, baby giraffe!
Lick, lick, lick!

Goodbye, baby elephant!
Squirt, squirt, squirt!

Goodbye, baby hippo!
Splish, splash, splosh!

Goodbye, baby parrot!
Squawk, squawk, squawk!

Goodbye, baby zebras!
Click-clack, click-clack!

Goodbye, baby leopard!
Raaaaaaaaaah!

Look at baby lion, cuddled up tight.
Purr very quietly and say night-night.

For Ella Rose
and Teddy – I.W.

For Mum – E.E.

First published 2006 by Macmillan Children's Books
an imprint of Pan Macmillan
20 New Wharf Road, London N1 9RR
Associated companies worldwide
www.panmacmillan.com

ISBN 978-1-5290-2733-4

Text copyright © Ian Whybrow 2006
Illustrations copyright © Edward Eaves 2006
Moral rights asserted.

1 3 5 7 9 8 6 4 2

A CIP catalogue record for this book is available from the British Library.

Printed in China